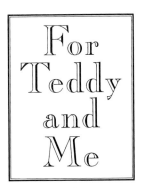

For Teddy and Me

D1391751

Little Rhymes
Chosen and Illustrated by
Prue Theobalds

Blackie   Bedrick/Blackie
London   New York

BLACKIE CHILDREN'S BOOKS

Penguin Books, Harmondsworth, Middlesex, England
Australia, Canada, New Zealand

First published 1993 as a mini edition
by Blackie Children's Books

A CIP catalogue record for this book is available
from the British Library
ISBN 0 216 940613

10 9 8 7 6 5 4 3 2 1

First US mini edition published 1993 by
Peter Bedrick Books
2112 Broadway
New York, NY 10023

Library of Congress Cataloging in Publication Data
is available for this book

ISBN 0 87226 514 5

Printed in Hong Kong by Wing King Tong Co Ltd

Contents

For Simon, Kate and Jo

Nursery rhymes are part of childhood and it is with great delight that each generation passes them on to the next. In this book I make no apology for changing the texts slightly here and there to encompass the teddy bear theme, for, as Peter Opie wrote in his introduction to *The Oxford Nursery Rhyme Book*, oral tradition recognises no 'correct' versions. We are all indebted to Iona and Peter Opie for keeping the oral tradition alive with their comprehensive collections and I would like to thank Iona Opie for her kind permission to reprint the rhymes on pages 8 and 10, which first appeared in *The Puffin Book of Nursery Rhymes*.

Some friends and relations may recognise their bears in various disguises on the following pages. If so, I hope they will not be offended by any liberties I might have taken. I have included some tickling, hand-clapping and finger-play rhymes which call for family involvement, and it is to my first grandchild and her family that this book is lovingly dedicated.

Pat-a-cake, pat-a-cake, baker's man,
Bake me a cake as fast as you can;
Pat it and prick it and mark it with T,
And put it in the oven for Teddy and me.

Lazy Zany Addlepate,
Go to bed early and get up late.

Two fat gentlemen
Met in a lane,
Bowed most politely,
Bowed once again.
How do you do?
How do you do?
How do you do again?

Jeremiah Obadiah, puff, puff, puff,
When he gives his messages he
    snuffs, snuffs, snuffs,
When he goes to school by day he
    roars, roars, roars,
When he goes to bed at night he
    snores, snores, snores,
When he goes to Christmas treat he
    eats plum-duff,
Jeremiah Obadiah,
    puff, puff, puff.

One, two, three, four,
Teddy at the cottage door,
Five, six, seven, eight,
Eating cherries off a plate.
Tinker, tailor, soldier, sailor,
Rich man, poor man, beggar man, thief.

Round and round the garden
Like a teddy bear;
One step, two steps . . .
Tickle you under there!

If you are to be a gentleman,
As I suppose you'll be,
You'll neither laugh nor smile
At the tickling of your knee.

Lavender's blue, dilly dilly,
Lavender's green,
When I am king, dilly dilly,
You shall be queen.

Ring-a-ring o'roses,
A pocket full of posies.
A-tishoo! A-tishoo!
We all fall down.

Here we go round the mulberry bush,
The mulberry bush, the mulberry bush;
Here we go round the mulberry bush,
On a cold and frosty morning.

Rain on the green grass,
Rain on the tree,
Rain on the house-top
But not on me!

Teddy bear, teddy bear, turn around.
Teddy bear, teddy bear, touch the ground.
Teddy bear, teddy bear, go upstairs.
Teddy bear, teddy bear, say your prayers.
Teddy bear, teddy bear, switch off the light.
Teddy bear, teddy bear, say goodnight.

Here am I,
Little Jumping Joan;
When nobody's with me
I'm all alone.

Handy Pandy, Jack-a-Dandy,
Loved plum cake and sugar candy;
He bought some at a baker's shop,
And then he came out,
Hop, hop, hop!

Teddy be nimble,
Teddy be quick,
Teddy jump over
The candle stick.

Little Tommy Tucker
Sings for his supper;
What shall we give him?
White bread and butter.

Pease porridge hot,
Pease porridge cold,
Pease porridge in the pot
Nine days old.

To market, to market,
To buy a plum bun;
Home again, home again,
Market is done.

Have you seen the muffin man,
The muffin man, the muffin man,
Have you seen the muffin man,
That lives in Drury Lane?

Teddy Hall
Is so small,
A rat could eat him,
Hat and all.

A sailor went to sea, sea, sea,
To see what he could see, see, see,
But all that he could see, see, see,
Was the bottom of the deep blue
    sea, sea, sea.

Rock-a-bye baby on the tree top,
When the wind blows the cradle will rock;
When the bough breaks the cradle will fall,
Down will come baby, cradle and all.

Twinkle, twinkle little star,
How I wonder what you are,
Up above the world so high,
Like a diamond in the sky.

Good night, sweet repose,
Lie on your back and not on your nose.
Half the bed and all the clothes,
Good night, sweet repose.